My name is Min-young, a regular woman in my thirties living in South Korea.

When I was a kid, my dad lost everything in the stock market. Every last dime. My mom, disgusted with him, ran off with another man. At first, I was ashamed—humiliated, even. I used to wish I had been born into a normal family, one where parents didn't scream at each other over dinner, where home wasn't a battlefield.

But as I got older, I realized... everyone's got their own mess. Divorced parents? Not exactly rare. Families who stay together just to make each other miserable? Plenty of those too. Turns out, my family wasn't that special after all. Just... average. Right?

My sister sure didn't think so. She moved out early, said she wanted nothing to do with this house. And you know what? She actually did fine on her own. Thrived, even. Watching her, I thought, *That's it. That's what I need to do. Get out, start my own family, and do it right this time.* No screw-ups like my dad. No regrets like my mom. I'd have the perfect home. The perfect life.

At least, that's what I believed.

Then, in my mid-twenties, my little brother—barely twenty years old—walked through the door with his girlfriend. Said she was pregnant. Said they were keeping the baby.

How the hell was he starting a family before me?

Mom lost her mind. Screamed at him to break up with her. Said there was no way they were having that baby. And just like that, my brother was gone. Walked out and never looked back.

I don't even know if he ended up having the kid. If they stayed together. If he's even alive. It's been years since we last heard from him.

But hey, doesn't every family have that one kid—the black sheep, the problem child, the one no one talks about anymore?

You Are Mine: A Dark and Twisted Thriller About Love, Obsession, and the Fight for Control

Bella Gu

Published by Bella Gu, 2025.

This is a work of fiction. Similarities to real people, places, or events are entirely coincidental.

YOU ARE MINE: A DARK AND TWISTED THRILLER ABOUT LOVE, OBSESSION, AND THE FIGHT FOR CONTROL

First edition. February 5, 2025.

Copyright © 2025 Bella Gu.

ISBN: 979-8230239390

Written by Bella Gu.

Table of Contents

Introduction 1
Chapter 1: My First Boyfriend 3
Chapter 2: The Tighter I Hold, The More I Lose.......................... 5
Chapter 3: Why Are You Changing?... 7
Chapter 4 : The Birth of Obsession 9
Chapter 5: The Möbius Loop 11
Chapter 6 : Our 'Real' Last Time... 13
Chapter 7: I Won't Lose You... 15
Chapter 8 : Shattered Heart, Filling the Cracks 19
Chapter 9 : Can Love Be Replaced?.. 23
Chapter 10 : Cracks in the Mask... 25
Chapter 11 : The Chains of Love 27
Chapter 12 : We're Truly in Love 29
Chapter 13 : The Mask | of the Perfect Daughter-in-Law 31
Chapter 14: The Shadow of a Broken Family............................. 35
Chapter 15: The Proof in the Whispers 37
Chapter 16 : The Weight of Evidence 39
Chapter 17 : Abandoned at the Door 43
Chapter 18 : The Art of Keeping a Family 47
Chapter 19: Come Back to Me.. 51
Chapter 20 : Forever, Just You and Me 55
Chapter 21 : Our True Beginning.. 57
Chapter 22: Perfect Love 61
Chapter 23: Happiness.. 63

Chapter 1: My First Boyfriend

I Never Knew What Love Felt Like

I never knew what it felt like to be loved. No—if I'm being honest, it's more accurate to say I never *got* to experience it.

At home, my parents were too busy tearing each other apart to care about me. There was no warmth, no gentle words—just endless fights and the suffocating weight of walking on eggshells. Love? That was something other people had. Something I watched from a distance, wondering if it was ever meant for me. But even so, I *wanted* to be loved.

Maybe not love, exactly, but at least the feeling of being *needed*. So, from a young age, I started telling little lies to get attention. Nothing big—just harmless things, like, *"My dad runs a business and makes a ton of money,"* or *"My mom always tells me I'm the prettiest girl she's ever seen."* Small, meaningless lies. But the thing about lies is that they pile up. And eventually, they come crashing down.

It happened in high school.

Every day during breaks, my friends would sit in a circle, talking about their boyfriends—gushing about sweet messages, surprise gifts, stolen kisses. At first, I just listened, nodding and laughing in all the right places. But the more I sat there, the more restless I became. I was the *only* one who had nothing to share.

So, I lied.

"Oh, this?" I said one day, pulling my wallet from my bag and setting it on the desk. *"My boyfriend gave it to me."*

It wasn't true. I had bought it myself with my own pocket money. But that didn't matter, right? Everyone exaggerates sometimes.

Or at least, that's what I thought.

But lies don't last forever.

Someone found out. And the moment they did, it wasn't just that I didn't have a boyfriend—it was that *everything* I had said was a lie. I wasn't just a girl without a boyfriend. I was a liar.

And suddenly, the people who used to sit beside me started avoiding me.

"They were all just pretending to care about me anyway."

That's what I told myself. That's what I *tried* to believe. But the truth? It hurt.

Then came college.

I studied hard, made it into a decent university, convinced myself this was my fresh start. Maybe here, I could be different. Maybe here, I could finally become someone who mattered.

And for a while, it felt like I was right.

It happened at a department mixer.

We were at a karaoke bar, the energy high, drinks flowing, voices filling the room. And then, in the middle of it all, a guy walked up to me. He sat beside me, leaned in slightly, and with a playful grin, he said—

"You're really cute."

Four simple words.

But they stuck.

I'd never been loved before. Never been *wanted*. But even without experience, I could tell—this was interest. This was attraction.

And it was thrilling.

No one had ever looked at me like that before. No one had ever made me feel *special*.

"Is this love?"

It was my first time feeling something like this. It was overwhelming, intoxicating.

I wanted more.

And once I had it, there was one thing I knew for certain—

I was never going to let it go.

Chapter 2: The Tighter I Hold, The More I Lose

I lied again. Not because I wanted to deceive him, but because I needed to keep him.

In my version of reality, I had the perfect family—a loving mother and father, a strong, independent sister, a responsible younger brother. A home filled with warmth. Stability. Love.

Of course, none of it was true. But what did it matter? It's not like we were getting married. It's not like he'd ever find out. Everyone tells little lies in relationships. This was just another one of those.

So I played my part. I acted like someone who had grown up with love, someone who knew how to give it in return. Someone who could care for others deeply and unconditionally. I thought that if I pretended long enough, it might actually become real. Maybe I could *become* that person. Maybe, for once, I could *deserve* to be loved.

And maybe, that's why he started falling for me. Day by day, I could feel it. He called me warm. He said I was always positive, that I radiated love. And I believed him. For the first time, I felt... *right*. Safe inside the version of myself he saw. Someone bright. Someone good. Someone worth loving.

I couldn't lose that. I *wouldn't* lose that.

So I held on tighter.

At first, it was just affection. I wanted to see him, to be with him, to spend every possible moment by his side. But then the feeling grew. Bigger. Darker. It started with little things. A gnawing discomfort whenever he was away. A twisting sensation in my stomach when I imagined him with someone else. A sudden wave of panic when I realized how easily he could leave me.

What if he met someone better? What if he was already talking to someone else? What if he didn't love me as much as I loved him?

So I watched. Checked his social media. Tracked his online status. Monitored the timestamps on his messages. Scrolled through the posts he liked, the accounts he followed.

"What did you do today?" I'd ask, my voice light, casual.

If he didn't reply quickly, I felt my chest tighten. *Why isn't he answering? Who is he with? Why is he ignoring me?*

One evening, he looked at me and sighed.

"Why do you ask so many questions these days?"

The words hit me like a slap. I was just curious. I just cared. I just wanted to know him better. But his expression was different that day. His voice, his eyes—there was something in them I hadn't seen before. Was it exhaustion? Had I become too much?

Maybe I should've stopped then. Maybe that was the moment to let go.

But I couldn't. I wouldn't.

"I ask because I love you," I told him.

He smiled. And I exhaled.

That's when I realized—love was the most powerful weapon I had. If I told him how much I loved him, he would feel guilty. He would try harder. He would reassure me. And he did. After that day, he messaged me more. Checked in more often. Called me before I even had to ask. I was satisfied.

For now.

"Love takes effort." That's what people say, right?

But what if I was the only one trying? What if he didn't want me as much as I wanted him? What if, little by little, he started to slip away? And if that happened... What would I do?

Chapter 3: Why Are You Changing?

I needed to know where he was, what he was doing. No—*I had* to know.

Why? Because love takes effort. Love means caring. Love means paying attention. Isn't that what love is? You don't just give it—you receive it too. If I cared about him, he should care about me just as much. That's how it's supposed to work.

But he didn't.

The replies that once came within minutes started taking an hour, then two. *I was busy. I was tired.* That's what he'd say. And I tried to understand. I really did. Or at least, I pretended to. But the more I told myself it was fine, the deeper the unease settled in my chest.

He used to ask about me first. Now, my curiosity annoyed him.

I needed to know why. Because if he *really* loved me, he wouldn't change.

Then, one day, he looked me in the eye and said it.

"I can't do this anymore, Min-young. You always check where I am, what I'm doing. Even when I'm home, you're watching me through social media, tracking when I'm online. It's too much. It's exhausting. Please... can you stop?"

I couldn't breathe.

My love... is exhausting?

That didn't make sense. I was doing what any loving girlfriend would do. I was making an effort. I was doing everything right.

Then why—why was he acting like I was the problem?

Maybe he was the one who changed.

But I held back. I swallowed the words burning inside me. I forced a smile, forced the corners of my lips to curve upwards like I wasn't falling apart.

"I'm sorry," I whispered, my voice barely steady.

"I guess I just love you too much... I was being foolish. I'll be better. I promise."

He exhaled in relief, nodded, and smiled softly.

That should've been the end of it. That should've been enough.

But something inside me twisted.

You were the one who called me cute first. You were the one who came to me.
And now you're saying it's too much?
People don't just change like that.
Or do they?
Is love supposed to change?
Or was I the only one truly in love?

Chapter 4 : The Birth of Obsession

I knew he had changed. No—I was *sure* of it.

One night, as I scrolled through his social media with my alternate account, something caught my eye. A comment from a girl I didn't recognize. Short, casual, but something about it felt *off*. There was an ease in her words, a familiarity in her tone. A joke, an inside reference—something that existed between *them* but not between *us*. And the way he responded? Playful. Comfortable.

Like they had a history.

Like she *meant* something.

"*Who the hell is this? What's going on between them?*"

That was the moment I started digging.

I found her profile. Then her friends. Then their comments, their tags, their interactions. Social media gives away more than people realize. Within minutes, I knew her school, her major, where she worked. And suddenly, everything made sense. *This* was why he had changed. *She* was the reason he was pulling away from me.

And soon enough, I got the confirmation I needed.

I was on my way home from class when I saw them.

Him. And *her.*

Walking side by side. Laughing. As if they'd always belonged together.

My heart dropped. A sharp, piercing weight in my chest. My vision blurred, and my breath came out in short, ragged gasps. A buzzing sound filled my ears. My hands started shaking. *So this is what betrayal feels like.*

"*I knew it. I fucking knew it.*"

I pulled out my phone and texted him.

"*How could you do this to me? How could love just change like that?*"

No reply.

Minutes passed. Then an hour. The message remained unread.

I could feel it—my blood boiling, my mind spiraling, my entire body tensing with rage. Was this it? Was love really this fragile? Was I that easy to discard? Or had he never really loved me at all?

But then I thought—*No.*

This wasn't the end. This was an opportunity. A chance to make our bond even stronger.

"I can't lose him."

"I won't lose him."

So I did what I had to do.

"I can't live without you."

"You can't do this to me."

"If you leave me, I have nothing left."

"I swear to God, I will die because of you."

The words poured out of me, desperate, raw, shaking with emotion. And the longer I spoke, the more real they became. At some point, I wasn't even sure if I was lying anymore.

Then, his name flashed on my screen.

I answered immediately.

His voice was frantic, laced with fear.

"Min-young, please. Stop. Don't say things like that. I'm sorry, okay? I swear, I won't talk to any other girls. I won't do anything to make you feel like this again. Just... please, don't say things like that."

That was when it hit me.

"Oh."

"So this is how I keep him."

If I threatened to disappear, he would cling to me. If I held my own life over his head, he would never leave.

And that was fine.

Because I *did* love him.

And love meant never letting go.

Chapter 5: The Möbius Loop

That was when it started—the rollercoaster ride we called love.

He kept breaking his promises. And every time he did, I got angry, disappointed, desperate. So I did the only thing I knew would work. I threatened to leave, threatened to disappear, threatened to *die*. And just like that, he'd snap back into focus, eyes only on me, too afraid to walk away.

But the pattern never changed.

He kept slipping, and I kept tightening my grip.

And every time, I had to go further than before.

One night, he showed up at my door, drunk. His eyes were bloodshot, his steps unsteady. He looked exhausted. Not just physically, but in a way that ran deeper, like something inside him had burned out. He stared at me for a long time before finally speaking.

"*Min-young... You have to stop saying that. Every time we fight, every time something goes wrong, you say you'll kill yourself. Do you have any idea what that does to me? Maybe you don't mean it, but I can't just ignore it. It's not fair. It's not... normal. Please. I'm begging you. Stop.*"

For a moment, I almost laughed.

Didn't everyone say things like that when they were angry? "*Do you want to die?*"—people threw that around all the time. It was just another phrase, another outburst, like cursing when you stub your toe. I had only taken it a little more seriously than most.

But he wasn't joking.

He looked *tired*.

And for the first time, I felt... something. Maybe guilt. Maybe pity.

Maybe even a little fear.

So I thought, *Fine. If it matters to him that much, I'll try. I'll hold back.*

And I did. For a while. But we all know how that goes.

People don't change that easily. If they do, it just means they're about to die.

I lasted a few days. I swallowed my words. I bit my tongue. Even when fights escalated, even when I wanted to scream, I held back. It was agonizing. My chest felt tight, my head buzzed, my whole body *itched* to release the words pressing against my throat.

This is love. This is how I love.

So why wasn't I allowed to say it?

And then, just like that, it slipped.

Not by choice. Not intentionally. It just *happened*.

The argument got worse. My breathing turned shallow. My vision blurred with rage. And before I could stop myself—

"Do you want me to die?"

"Stop."

"I'll do it."

"Don't."

It kept looping, over and over. A Möbius strip of the same words, repeating endlessly.

"Do you want me to die?"

"Stop."

"I'll do it."

"Don't."

Fighting. Crying. Threats. Pleas. And then exhaustion. We would tell ourselves *next time* would be different. That we would try harder, love better, fix what was broken.

But it always ended the same way.

Maybe love was supposed to be like this.

Or maybe... it was just me.

Chapter 6 : Our 'Real' Last Time

For six years, we rode this rollercoaster.

Six years of fights and tears, breaking up and crawling back, looping in an endless cycle. In that time, I graduated, got a job, became an adult navigating the real world. He, on the other hand, took longer. He was studying for the civil service exam, delaying his career, and when he finally passed, he was assigned to a different city—an hour away.

Not far enough to call it long distance, but just far enough to feel the distance creeping in.

Still, we held on.

Weekdays were for our separate lives, but weekends belonged to us. Every Friday, I'd drive to his apartment, because he never came to me. His place was always a mess, clothes thrown everywhere, dishes stacked in the sink. And I cleaned. Every. Single. Time.

But that was fine. That was *normal*. That was what you did for someone you loved.

Then one day, on a weekday, I missed him so much it physically hurt. I don't even know why. It wasn't logical, it wasn't reasonable—I just *needed* to see him.

So I left work early. Took half a day off. Got in my car and drove straight to his place, thinking I'd surprise him. Thinking it would be cute.

He wasn't home when I arrived. Of course he wasn't—he was still at work. But I didn't call him. I wanted to keep it a surprise.

I stepped inside, inhaling the familiar scent of his apartment. The space I had practically made into a second home. I set my bag down, tied my hair up, and started cleaning, like always. Wiped the counters, threw out the trash, straightened the blankets, restocked the fridge. Then, as I was organizing his dresser, something slipped out of the drawer.

A condom. Neatly folded inside its transparent wrapper, perfectly intact, untouched.

I stared at it, my mind stalling like a car engine that refused to turn over.

"What... the hell?"

My body moved before my brain could catch up.

I picked it up, turned it over in my hands, trying to rationalize what I was seeing.

I took birth control. I had been on it for *years*. We never used condoms. *Never.*

Then why... was there one here?

My heart pounded so hard it hurt.

Maybe he bought it just in case. A spare, for some hypothetical moment, an impulse purchase at a convenience store. *That's reasonable, right? That could happen, right?*

But no. That didn't make sense.

I started looking around, really looking.

And suddenly, everything was different.

A piece of clothing on the chair that wasn't his. A bottle of shampoo in the bathroom that smelled *wrong*. A faint smudge on the mirror, like someone had leaned too close.

It had all been there. Right in front of me. The whole time.

I just hadn't wanted to see it.

"Fuck."

Something inside me cracked, splintering so deep I could almost hear it.

Chapter 7: I Won't Lose You

For the first hour, I sat in stunned silence.

The second hour, I cursed until my throat burned.

By the third hour, I was tearing through his apartment like a detective unraveling a crime scene.

I searched everywhere—his desk, his drawers, under the bed, inside his bags, even the damn trash can. I *had* to know. I needed to see the evidence, to find out who the hell he had been fucking behind my back.

And then, as if fate wanted to twist the knife even deeper, I found it.

His computer. Logged in. Messenger wide open.

"Gotcha."

My fingers trembled as I moved the mouse. And there it was—months of messages, playful banter, late-night flirting. The same hands that once held me, touched me, loved me... had been reaching for someone else all along.

She worked in his office.

It had been going on for *months.*

Maybe even longer.

Six years. I had spent six years with this man. Six years of driving down every weekend to see him. Six years of picking up after him, loving him, making him my whole fucking world. And he—he had been in love with someone else.

"You really thought I wouldn't find out?"

I inhaled sharply, but before I could even let that breath out, my body was already moving. I grabbed my keys. My vision tunneled.

The next thing I knew, I was in my car, speeding toward his office.

[At His Workplace]

"Oh? Min-young? What are you doing h—"

"You filthy son of a bitch. You fucked her, didn't you?"

Silence.

His face went pale. The room went still. His coworkers—people I'd never met, people who didn't know a damn thing about me—stared in stunned disbelief. The air shifted, heavy, suffocating.

But I didn't care. I only saw him. Or rather, *it*.

Because he wasn't my boyfriend anymore.

He was just a disgusting, lying piece of shit.

"Listen up, everyone!"

I took a deep breath and raised my hand high. The fluorescent lights overhead reflected off the object I was holding, making it unmistakably clear.

"Do you see this? Do you know what this is?"

Gasps. A few murmurs. Some turned away, pretending they hadn't heard me.

"This was in his apartment." I laughed, breathless. *"But funny thing—I take birth control. We haven't used one of these in years. So tell me, why the hell was this in his drawer?"*

Silence.

"I'll tell you why. Because he's been screwing someone else. Probably that slut over there. Isn't that right?"

A ripple of chaos spread through the office. People whispering, shifting uncomfortably. Some tried to intervene, their hands reaching for me, trying to de-escalate.

But I wasn't done.

"You pathetic bastard." My voice trembled—not from sadness, but from pure, undiluted rage. *"I gave you everything. I loved you. I fucking devoted my life to you. And this is how you repay me?"*

Still, he said nothing. He just stood there—stiff, frozen, like a deer caught in headlights.

"Say something, you coward!"

He swallowed hard. *"Min-young... please, stop."*

"Stop?" I let out a sharp, humorless laugh. *"You're telling me to stop?!"*

More hands on my arms. More voices begging me to calm down. But the more they tried to contain me, the louder I got.

"Why should I be the one to calm down? Huh? If this happened to you, would you just stand there and take it? Would you smile and walk away?!"

And then, for the first time since I walked in, our eyes met.

I expected guilt. Regret. *Anything* to show he was sorry.

But what I saw instead?
Fear.
Real, genuine *fear.*
And that was when I knew—I had finally gotten through to him.
I smiled.
"Yeah. Now you get it, don't you?"

Chapter 8 : Shattered Heart, Filling the Cracks

After that day, he left me only one message.
"I'm sorry. Let's end this."
One sentence. That was all.
And then he cut me off completely—phone, texts, social media, even email. Every possible connection severed in an instant, like I had never existed in his life.
It was almost funny. Or at least, it should have been.
Guilt made him run? How convenient. How pathetic.
But still. Still.
No matter how much I told myself he was the coward, no matter how much I cursed his name, the truth sat heavy in my chest like a stone, pressing down, refusing to budge.
I had seen it with my own eyes. The man I loved—*the only person I had ever truly loved*—had shared his body, his time, his thoughts with someone else.
And now, there was nothing left of us.
The sound of my heart breaking wasn't loud. It wasn't dramatic. It was silent and suffocating, like a slow, crushing weight I couldn't push off.
I didn't know what to do with it. The pain. The emptiness.
I had friends. Good people. But telling them? Confessing the full extent of my humiliation? That was out of the question. If I admitted how much it hurt, it would only make me *weaker*. They would pity me. They would see me as *pathetic*.
No. This was something I had to endure alone.
But I didn't know how.
So I did what anyone drowning in heartbreak would do.
I opened YouTube.
In the search bar, I typed: *"How to get over a breakup."*
For a few minutes, I just stared at the screen, my finger hovering over the play button.
It was embarrassing. The kind of thing only desperate people did.

But I hit play anyway.

"The best way to get over someone is to move on with someone new."

That sentence lodged itself into my mind, repeating over and over.

If a shattered window needs filling, then it only makes sense to patch the cracks with something else.

Yes. That made sense.

I didn't need to sit in this emptiness, drowning in thoughts of him.

I needed *someone else*.

So, I got started.

The World of Dating Apps

Lately, dating apps had become *the* way to meet people. I had seen the ads, read the testimonials. *Find love. Find fun. Find whatever you're looking for.*

Perfect.

I downloaded all of them—A, B, C, every app with a decent reputation. If I was going to do this, I needed efficiency. Love wasn't the goal. Survival was.

The first step was the profile.

I wasn't unattractive, but I wasn't going to take any chances. I carefully selected my best photos, ran them through filters, adjusted the lighting, subtly smoothed out imperfections. A slightly better version of myself—it was just what people did. No one was *honest* about their real face.

Then, the bio.

Not too much. Just enough. A balance of humor, intelligence, and warmth.

Truth wasn't necessary.

Everyone wore a mask in this game, and I wasn't going to be the only one showing my real face.

"Looking for someone to fill the emptiness."

I typed the words, then hit save.

I didn't have to wait long.

Notifications flooded in. Matches, messages, profiles swiping right. My phone wouldn't stay quiet.

Every ping, every alert, felt like a drop of water on cracked, dry earth. Filling the spaces. Soothing the ache.

"This is... easy?"

Dozens of names, faces, conversations. Some dull, some interesting.

Then, one day, *he* appeared.

A message. A face I liked. My type.
This was it. The real distraction was about to begin.

Chapter 9 : Can Love Be Replaced?

As we talked, I realized how much we had in common. Favorite foods, dislikes, hobbies—everything seemed to align effortlessly. The more we spoke, the stronger the feeling grew. This wasn't just a simple conversation; it was the beginning of something new.

7 PM. Café A.

He was already there, sitting at a corner table. A single flower in his hand, waiting for me.

As I walked toward him, he looked up and smiled. A warm, genuine smile—one that made my chest tighten in a way I hadn't felt in a long time.

And just like that, the lingering shadows of my ex disappeared.

He was a clean slate. A fresh start. Someone who could rewrite everything that had been ruined before.

We talked for hours, our conversation flowing seamlessly. At some point, the topic of family came up.

I did what I always did—I painted the perfect picture.

A loving home. Parents who adored each other. A strong, independent older sister. A responsible younger brother.

Was it the truth? No.

But if I said it enough, maybe it could be. Maybe I could make it real.

He listened attentively, nodding along.

"My family is the same way," he said. *"My parents are still crazy about each other, and my siblings and I are really close."*

A thought struck me like lightning.

Was this fate? Were we meant to be?

Everything lined up too perfectly—our interests, our upbringing, the way our conversations felt effortless.

Could I really have found someone this easily?

Just as my mind began racing, he looked straight into my eyes and spoke.

"Min-young, we have so much in common. Everything just feels... right. I know we haven't known each other for long, but I think getting to know each other more is something we can do while being together."

He leaned in slightly.

"What do you think? Should we start dating?"

For a moment, my mind went blank.

He was choosing me. He wanted me.

A new beginning, handed to me just like that.

Excitement bubbled up in my chest.

"Yes. This feels right. This time, I'll get it right."

I reached for his hand, my fingers lacing through his.

"Yes, let's start today."

And then, a thought crept in—soft, subtle, but impossible to ignore.

"Maybe... just maybe... this is the person who will finally give me the perfect family I've always wanted."

Chapter 10 : Cracks in the Mask

I swore I wouldn't repeat my past mistakes. I promised myself—*this time, I'll do it right. No slip-ups, no patterns, no losing control.*

So, I put on a mask.

I became the perfect girlfriend. The understanding, easygoing, supportive woman every man would want. I laughed off little things, never got jealous, never asked too many questions. I played my role flawlessly.

But beneath the mask, nothing had changed.

When he wasn't looking, I was still *me.*

I monitored his life carefully—who he spent time with, where he went, who he kept in touch with. I didn't question him openly. I never let my curiosity show. I was patient, meticulous, careful.

And it worked.

For three years, everything went smoothly. We were happy, stable. And when the time came, we took the next step. Wedding venues were booked, preparations were made.

Everything was perfect.

This time, things were going exactly the way I wanted.

Until one night. That night, I found myself staring at his phone records.

I wasn't even looking for anything. It was just a habit—an old reflex. But then, I saw it.

A name. *"Kim Hyeji."*

I blinked. Where had I heard that before?

My fingers clenched around the phone as my mind scrambled for an answer. Why was there a *woman's* name in his call log? And why the hell had they talked for *five minutes?*

I could feel my heart pounding. *Think, Min-young. Think.*

And then, it clicked.

A long time ago, he had mentioned an office relationship. A woman he used to date when he worked at his old company.

Her name was— *"Kim Hyeji."*
A cold, sharp realization sank into my gut.
"Son of a bitch."
The curse slipped from my lips before I could stop it. The mask was slipping.

Chapter 11 : The Chains of Love

I didn't hold back. I shook him awake, yanking him from his sleep. His eyes barely opened as he blinked at me, confused and groggy.

"Why the hell is her name on your call log?"

"Why the fuck are you talking to Hyeji?"

His confusion quickly turned into alarm. He sat up, rubbing his face as if trying to process what was happening. Then he gave me the most pathetic excuse I had ever heard.

"Min-young, calm down... It's nothing. My sister is best friends with Hyeji's older sister, so... I can't completely cut ties with her. It was just a casual check-in. Nothing more. Don't overthink it."

"Don't overthink it?"

"It's nothing?"

I felt something inside me snap.

"Don't give me that fucking bullshit."

My mind went blank. My lungs clenched like they couldn't pull in air. My heart pounded so hard it felt like my ribs would crack under the pressure. My vision blurred.

And then—I saw the window. A single thought ran through my head.

"If I jump now, will this pain stop?"

"If I just end everything, will I finally escape this nightmare?"

Would he finally *get it*? Would he finally understand what it felt like to be me?

I walked toward the window, my legs moving on their own. The cold night air seeped through the tiny gap in the frame. I reached for it, hoisting one foot onto the sill.

His eyes widened in terror.

"Min-young, stop! What are you doing? Please, don't!"

He lunged at me, grabbing my arms. His hands were shaking—desperate, terrified. *Good.*

That's how it should be.

"If you didn't want this to happen, you shouldn't have done it."

I stared at him, my grip tightening around his trembling hands. His face had turned deathly pale. The way he was looking at me—like I was a ticking bomb, like one wrong move and I'd explode—was satisfying.

This is love. Love is power. Love is who controls who.

"Hey," I whispered, tilting my head slightly, letting my voice soften into something fragile, something delicate. *"When I found out you were still talking to your ex, I wanted to die. I couldn't breathe. My heart felt like it was being ripped apart."*

I leaned in just a little closer, just enough for him to feel my breath against his skin.

"If I'm in this much pain, are you still going to keep talking to her?"

His lips parted, but no words came out. His entire body shook. Then, after what felt like an eternity, he exhaled shakily and whispered:

"No. I won't. I swear. Never again. I'm sorry. I'm so sorry."

A slow, satisfied smile curled on my lips.

"Good."

That's right. He wasn't going anywhere. He was mine. He would always be mine.

Love isn't about compromise. Love isn't about fairness. Love is about possession. And I?

I don't let go of what's mine.

Chapter 12 : We're Truly in Love

After the stormy night that nearly shattered everything, our wedding day crept closer. Everything had to be perfect. Everything had to look flawless. At least on the surface.

It was around this time that I ran into an old friend, Dokyung. She was one of the few people I considered *close*—or at least, close enough.

"Min-young! How's the wedding planning going? You must be so happy these days!"

Her face beamed with excitement, her voice filled with that naive enthusiasm people had when they still believed in fairytales. I inhaled slowly, curled my lips into the sweetest smile, and let my voice drip with the perfect amount of contentment.

"*Oh, you know~ I'm practically dying of happiness~ My fiancé is such a devoted guy. He's all about work and home, work and home—such a homebody, really. And he's been handling most of the wedding prep so perfectly that I barely have anything to do!*"

Of course, that wasn't entirely true. But a little exaggeration never hurt.

And when I saw the flicker of envy in Dokyung's eyes, the satisfaction hit me like a warm sip of coffee on a cold day. That subtle shift in expression—the one that said *you're above me, you're winning*—was enough to make my mood soar.

"*Wow, really? That's amazing. I'm so jealous~*"

Yes. That's how it should be.

"*Oh! By the way, I got a boyfriend recently! We should totally do a double date sometime! I'd love to introduce you two!*"

My smile twitched for half a second before I caught myself.

"*Oh? That sounds fun! What does he do? Is he good-looking?*"

"*Yeah, he owns a café. And his coffee? Seriously the best I've ever had. He's super charming too. I actually asked him for his number first! Felt so empowering, you know?*"

A café owner?

My brain did a quick calculation. Café owners made more than government employees, right? Which meant her boyfriend potentially made more than my soon-to-be husband.

So what, was she trying to flex? Was she subtly implying she scored better than me?

A spark of irritation ignited in my chest.

"Oh, really? That's nice~ Actually, my fiancé just got me a new car! Since we're planning to have kids soon, he said driving a compact car wouldn't be safe, so he got me a bigger one. Said he wanted me to have something safer and more luxurious~"

I made sure to stretch out my words just enough to let them settle in.

"Wow, that's so thoughtful of him! He's really got a big heart!"

Of course. That's right.

You don't get to outshine me.

I lifted my coffee cup and took a slow sip, relishing the moment.

Stay where you belong. Beneath me.

Chapter 13 : The Mask of the Perfect Daughter-in-Law

The wedding went off without a hitch, and we settled into our new life as a picture-perfect newlywed couple. But along with the title of *wife*, I also inherited another role—*daughter-in-law*.

And I had to be the best at it.

"Mother, it must be lonely at home with Taehyun away so often. I'll make sure to visit whenever you're feeling bored! We live so close anyway, so if you ever want company, just call me. Or better yet, I'll just come by myself!"

"Oh, no need, dear. You two should enjoy your time together as newlyweds. But thank you for saying that. It means a lot."

Hearing those words made my heart swell with satisfaction. Being praised, being appreciated—it was intoxicating. I believed that if I worked hard enough, I could *earn* love.

But not everyone seemed to think I deserved it.

One afternoon at my in-laws' house, Taehyun's younger sister threw a casual jab my way, her voice laced with something bitter.

"Minyoung, I know you spend a lot of time with our parents, but shouldn't you visit your own parents too? I mean, wouldn't they feel a little neglected?"

For a moment, my brain stalled. *What?*

I bent over backward to integrate myself into this family, went out of my way to please them, and now I had to hear this? I clenched my teeth behind a tight-lipped smile.

"Oh, of course! I visit them too when I can."

She smirked slightly, as if she had won some unspoken battle. That was the moment I realized—this wasn't just a casual comment. It was a test. A challenge.

Fine. If she wanted to play, I'd play.

A few weeks later, I was helping my mother-in-law prepare dinner. *The perfect daughter-in-law* had to be helpful in the kitchen, after all.

"*Mother, let me take care of a few extra side dishes today!*"

My mother-in-law smiled approvingly. That was all the encouragement I needed. I meticulously prepared the food, putting in more effort than I ever had before. But just as we set the dishes on the table, Taehyun's sister casually remarked,

"*Oh... Minyoung, you're not really used to making these kinds of dishes, are you?*"

I blinked. *Excuse me?*

"*I mean, they taste a little different from what Mom usually makes... Maybe it's just not to our usual family taste?*"

The air in the room shifted. My mother-in-law chuckled awkwardly, trying to smooth things over.

"*It's fine, dear. It's the effort that counts!*"

But my ears were already ringing.

I knew what she was doing.

"*Oh, really? Well, every family has different tastes! I'll keep that in mind for next time!*" I smiled sweetly, setting my chopsticks down.

I wouldn't forget this.

From that day on, I researched and perfected every dish I brought to the table. I wouldn't just cook; I'd create *art*. Traditional recipes, restaurant-level plating, even specialty dishes tailored to their supposed *family taste*.

I would never hear that insult again.

When the holidays approached, I prepared gifts for everyone. High-end red ginseng for my mother-in-law, premium whiskey for my father-in-law, and luxury hand creams for Taehyun's sisters. It had to be perfect.

But when I handed over the gifts, Taehyun's younger sister tilted her head, smiling in that *passive-aggressive* way of hers.

"Minyoung, you really didn't have to go all out like this... It's a bit much, don't you think?"

I forced a laugh.

"Oh, it's just a small token! We're family, after all."

She kept staring at me, then added,

"Mom doesn't really like things like this. You didn't waste money, did you?"

My fingers curled slightly.

Waste money?

After everything I'd done, *that's* her response?

This wasn't about generosity. This was a competition. A power struggle to see who held more influence in this family.

I smiled, keeping my voice light.

"Oh, then I'll exchange it for something she likes better! It's important that she gets something she truly enjoys, after all~"

But in my mind, the decision had already been made.

You started this war. Let's see who wins.

From that holiday forward, my gifts grew even grander. More expensive, more extravagant, more *undeniable*.

I didn't care what she thought anymore.

I just needed to be the most *beloved* in this family.

Every backhanded comment, every patronizing remark, every challenge she threw my way—I took note of them all.

Because this wasn't just about family.

This was about control.

And I wasn't about to lose.

"Alright, let's see how far you're willing to go."

Chapter 14: The Shadow of a Broken Family

Between wedding preparations, work, and endless household chores, my body had finally given in. I had gained nearly 20 kilograms since my office days. At first, I wondered if I might be pregnant, but no. It was nothing more than stress-induced binge eating.

Day by day, I could feel my body getting heavier. The numbers on the scale kept climbing, and the reflection in the mirror no longer resembled the person I used to be. But I didn't really care. What was the big deal? I was still me, and my health was fine.

But Taehyun thought differently.

"We need to start preparing for a baby, and I don't want you straining your body too much. Maybe losing a little weight would be good for you."

His words lingered in my head. I wasn't that overweight. My health was fine. So what exactly was the problem?

Then one day, Taehyun and I met up with Dokyung for brunch. She was excitedly talking about how she had recently started Pilates.

"It really helps with my posture, and I think I'm losing some weight too! More than that, I just feel healthier overall. Minyoung, you should give it a try! There's a great studio near your place. I swear, it makes a difference."

I barely paid attention, but Taehyun's reaction was different. His eyes lit up with interest as he turned to me, almost expectantly.

Shouldn't love mean staying the same, no matter what? Shouldn't he love me regardless of whether I gained or lost weight? Wasn't that what real love was?

After that day, Taehyun kept encouraging me to try Pilates. He didn't push too hard, but he brought it up often enough that I finally caved. I signed up for a class at a small studio in our apartment complex. I didn't particularly enjoy it, but I went—once, maybe twice a week—just enough to keep Taehyun from bringing it up again.

And then, like a miracle, we found out I was pregnant.

The moment I saw those two lines on the test strip, the world suddenly seemed brighter. I was finally going to build my own perfect family. Everything was falling into place. Taehyun looked just as happy as I was.

But the happiness didn't last.

The baby was gone before we even had the chance to meet them.

A **missed miscarriage.**

When the doctor said those words, my mind went blank. It felt like my entire body had been hollowed out. And in a way, it had.

All the excitement, all the anticipation—my future, my family, my happiness—had been shattered in an instant.

That word **miscarriage** drove me insane. I clung to Taehyun, sobbing uncontrollably.

"I don't think I can keep living. The baby is gone, and now... I have no reason to exist."

Taehyun grabbed my shoulders, his grip firm yet trembling. His eyes were desperate.

"Minyoung, please... Don't say that. What about me? If you say things like that... how am I supposed to keep going?"

I couldn't answer him.

I just sat there, staring blankly out the window.

What was I supposed to live for now?

Chapter 15: The Proof in the Whispers

Maybe it was because Taehyun had told his family about my condition. The in-laws, in an effort to be "supportive," suggested a healing retreat. A cozy pension in a lush, green countryside.

Healing? Don't make me laugh. There's no such thing as healing for a woman who just lost her child.

The moment we arrived, I regretted coming. My mood plummeted as soon as I saw Taehyun's younger sister eyeing me up and down, her expression laced with irritation.

I should've stayed home.

I decided I'd just lock myself in one of the rooms and stay in bed the entire trip. But, of course, Taehyun wouldn't let me be.

"You need to get out more," he insisted, grabbing my hand. "It'll help clear your head."

I didn't want to move. I didn't want to do anything. I just wanted to disappear under the covers and pretend the world didn't exist. But he never listened.

And then, out of the corner of my eye, I saw them.

The sisters, whispering to each other, stealing glances at me.

Those bitches. They were talking about me, weren't they?

I clenched my fists. No, I *knew* they were talking about me. But if I confronted them, I already knew what would happen.

"Oh no, you misunderstood! We weren't talking about you!"

Lies.

I needed proof.

Then, an idea struck me. What if I left my phone behind and recorded everything? I could set it down, screen hidden, and leave the voice recorder on. That way, while I was gone, their little gossip session would be recorded in real-time.

Yes. That would work.

Casually, I placed my phone on the coffee table, making sure the screen was facing down. Then, acting as if nothing was amiss, I followed Taehyun outside.

He chatted as we walked along the quiet forest path. I nodded absentmindedly, pretending to listen. But in truth, I couldn't hear a damn thing. My mind was elsewhere.

"Taehyun," I finally interrupted. "I'm exhausted. Can we head back now?"

"Huh? Oh... yeah, sure. It's about time for dinner anyway."

The second we stepped back into the pension, I grabbed my phone and pressed play.

"Minyoung... #@$@#..."

The moment I heard my name, my blood pressure spiked.

I didn't even need to listen to the rest. That was enough.

They *were* talking about me.

That was all the confirmation I needed.

With white-hot rage coursing through my veins, I stormed into the living room. There she was, Taehyun's younger sister, sitting there with a smug little smirk.

I didn't hesitate. I grabbed her hair, yanking her head back.

"Oh, go on. Keep talking," I sneered. "You seemed to have plenty to say when I wasn't around. Why don't you say it to my face now, huh? Come on, you spineless bitch!"

"Aaah! Minyoung, what the hell?!" she shrieked.

The older sister jumped up in shock, rushing over to pull me away, but I wasn't letting go.

No. I *couldn't* let go.

The entire room fell into stunned silence.

Taehyun. His parents. His entire family. All of them just stood there, frozen, staring at me like I was some kind of monster.

But I didn't care.

I *would not* be disrespected. I yanked harder, my voice shaking with fury.

"You had so much fun talking shit behind my back, but what? Now that I'm standing right here, you suddenly have nothing to say?"

"Are you insane?!" she screamed.

Maybe. Yeah. Maybe I was.

Chapter 16 : The Weight of Evidence

"You talked behind my back, didn't you? Here, I have proof!"

I pulled out my phone and hit play. The audio file filled the tense air as I stood in front of my in-laws, my hands gripping the device tightly.

This was it. The moment of truth. They would finally see that I wasn't crazy, that I wasn't overreacting.

But then...

"*Minyoung unni and Taehyun, where did they go? Are they outside? Oh, I guess they went sightseeing.*"

And that was it.

Silence. My breath hitched.

"...What?"

That's all? No insults, no mockery, no gossip? But they *must* have said something. They *must* have talked about me. I *knew* they did.

My hand, still holding the phone, slowly lowered.

Something was wrong. The way they were looking at me.

"Minyoung," my mother-in-law's voice cut through the room like a blade. "Did you just record our conversation?"

Her tone was low, cold, and dangerously sharp.

"You do realize how disturbing that is, don't you?"

Disturbing?

The word felt foreign, completely detached from reality. I needed proof. That's all. Proof that I wasn't imagining things, proof that I wasn't crazy. Why was that wrong?

Then Taehyun spoke, his voice eerily calm.

"Minyoung, you always threaten to kill yourself whenever we argue, and I've tried my best to be patient, to comfort you, to hold this marriage together. But this?" He gestured toward my phone, his face unreadable. "Bringing my entire family into it like this? I can't do this anymore."

A sinking feeling crept into my chest.

"Come outside for a minute."

His voice was gentle, but there was no warmth in it.

I followed him out of the living room, my heart pounding violently against my ribs.

Something felt off.

"Minyoung," he started, his eyes holding a distance I had never seen before, "do you realize how messed up this is? How completely irrational your actions have been?"

"What the hell do you mean by that?" My voice cracked.

I *had* to say something, had to justify myself.

"Your sister always talks shit about me! You *know* she does! I told you over and over, and now I finally tried to get proof, and suddenly *I'm* the problem? How does that make sense?!"

I could hear my own voice rising, shaking with a mix of frustration and desperation.

Taehyun sighed deeply, rubbing his temple like he was exhausted.

"Minyoung... you really don't see what's wrong, do you?"

His next words felt like a gunshot.

"I don't think I can do this anymore."

My ears started ringing.

"What?"

"I think we need to separate."

The words knocked the air out of my lungs.

"Are you serious?" My voice wavered. "You're really saying we should get a divorce over *this*? Over something so stupid? Divorce isn't like breaking up with a boyfriend, Taehyun! You don't just walk away like that!"

He shook his head. "This isn't sudden, Minyoung. I've been holding on, trying to make this work. But today... today was too much."

My hands clenched into fists. Then, the final blow.

"And honestly? I wasn't going to say this, but I think you should see someone. A doctor. A therapist. Just... get some help."

My stomach twisted violently.

A doctor? A therapist? He thought I was *insane*.

My own husband.

I felt my body go numb, all the anger and panic draining out of me.

"You're really labeling me as some kind of psycho over one recording?" My voice trembled. "You're making me sound like some kind of lunatic?"

Silence. That was all the confirmation I needed.

I scoffed, laughing bitterly.

"Unbelievable."

I looked him dead in the eyes, forcing myself to stay composed, to keep my voice steady.

"Fine. Let's do it."

His brows furrowed. "What?"

"Let's get a divorce," I said, my lips curling into a smile. "If that's what you want, then *fine*."

And the second I said it, I realized the truth.

This wasn't a fight.

This wasn't something we'd fix tomorrow or next week.

This was real.

This was *the end*.

Chapter 17 : Abandoned at the Door

Coming back home, my mind was in turmoil.
Divorce.
I never thought that word would come so close to my life. No—divorce was never supposed to be *in* my life. I wasn't the type of person who failed. I was supposed to have a perfect family. A perfect marriage. That was the plan.

And yet, here I was.

I kept replaying everything in my head. Was what I did *really* that bad? All I did was record a conversation for proof, yet Taehyun, his family, everyone—treated me like a monster. If I told this to Do-kyung or any of my friends, I was sure they'd say, *"That's it? What's the big deal?"*

So... what if I just apologized?

If I just said I was really sorry, if I showed them I regretted it—wouldn't they let it slide? Wouldn't things go back to how they were?

Convincing myself that was the answer, I decided to go see my sister-in-law first.

I stood outside her door and pressed the doorbell.
"It's me, Minyoung. Can we talk for a second?"
Silence. Not a single sound from inside.
Then—
"I have nothing to say to you."
Her voice was cold, detached.
"And Minyoung, don't come looking for me again. Actually, don't contact anyone in our family anymore."
Click.
The intercom went dead.

I thought about knocking, but my hand wouldn't move. No—it wasn't just that. My fingertips were trembling.

Was I really someone to be *stepped* on like this? What did I even do that was *so* wrong?

I clicked my tongue, glared at the door for a second, and turned away.

Fine. The sister-in-law was the problem from the start anyway. If I just apologized directly to his parents, maybe they'd understand.

I just needed to look *pathetic* enough. And honestly? It wasn't even an act. If I shared my difficult childhood, they'd *have* to feel a little sympathy, right?

So, I went to my in-laws' house.

Standing at the door, I pressed the bell.

"Mother, Father, it's me. Minyoung."

Silence.

Then, a single, short response.

"Go home. We have nothing to say to you."

I froze.

"Mother, Father... I'm really sorry. I..."

I stopped, took a deep breath. Right. *I need to sound vulnerable.*

"I... I never really got much love from my parents growing up."

I made my voice shake, just enough.

"They got divorced when I was little, and I had to grow up in a broken home. I never really knew what love was supposed to look like, or how to give it properly. That's why I messed up."

I paused, letting the weight of my words settle.

"I truly regret it, Mother. I swear, I do. I even went to see my sister-in-law just now to apologize."

A small, shaky sob escaped my lips. That should do it. *Older people always forgive in the end. They always say, "Let's just put this behind us."*

But—

Silence.

"Mother? Father?"

Nothing.

The quiet stretched on, pressing against my chest like a weight.

I licked my lips, my hands going clammy.

"I... I really am sorry. Please, just once, hear me out."

The intercom shut off.

I stood there, frozen.

My hands went ice-cold. No—my whole body did.

Was I *really* being tossed aside like this? Even after everything? Even after I *lowered* myself to this?

A wave of anger surged through me.

I clenched my fists and knocked on the door, harder this time.

"Mother, please! Just open the door! Mother!!!"

No one came.

And finally, I understood.

There was no one left in this house who would open the door for me.

I stood there for a long time, not moving. Not even thinking.

Eventually, my feet carried me away. The cold night air brushed against my face.

For the first time in my life, I felt like I had been completely, utterly abandoned.

Chapter 18 : The Art of Keeping a Family

I dragged my exhausted body back home, the weight of rejection pressing down on me.

Just hours ago, I had been standing in front of my in-laws' house, pleading for forgiveness. I had even let my tears fall, hoping for a shred of sympathy. But all I got in return was silence and a locked door.

Was I really that disposable? Had I become so insignificant that they could cast me aside without a second thought?

The real tragedy wasn't even that they had abandoned me. No, the real tragedy was that, even after everything, a part of me still believed that *maybe, just maybe, things could go back to the way they were.*

That illusion didn't last long.

Taehyun looked at me with an expression so calm it felt rehearsed.

"Minyoung, let's get a divorce."

I stared at him, unable to process his words.

"...What?"

"I want a divorce. We're both exhausted, and you know it."

I searched his face for a hint of hesitation, some sign that he didn't really mean it. But his expression was cold, detached—like he had already made up his mind.

"No." I said firmly. *"I'm not getting a divorce."*

"Minyoung, it's over. There's no way we can keep living like this. If you refuse a mutual divorce, I'll have no choice but to file for a contested one. And honestly... it'll only make things worse for you."

"...A contested divorce?"

"Yeah. If you won't agree, I'll take it to court. I already consulted a lawyer. They said I have more than enough grounds to win."

A lawyer? *Legal grounds?*

For the first time, my mind went blank. This wasn't just about feelings anymore. This wasn't a phase we could argue our way out of. Taehyun had already set things in motion.

"It'd be better for you to agree to this now."

Better for *me*?

"You're telling me to get divorced for my own sake?"

"Yes. If you fight this, it's only going to make things harder."

"Don't make me laugh." I scoffed, my voice sharp.

"What exactly did I do that was so unforgivable? Wanting to protect my family is a crime now? Loving you was a mistake?"

Taehyun let out a dry chuckle.

"Love? You think that was love?"

Something inside me cracked at the way he said it.

"It wasn't?"

"No, Minyoung. It wasn't."

He looked at me with something close to pity.

"You never really loved me. You just wanted to own me. To control me. You convinced yourself that your obsession was love, but it never was."

My breath hitched.

"Then what about you?" I snapped. *"Did you love me?"*

He hesitated.

That hesitation was all I needed to know.

Of course.

This wasn't just about the fights, or my so-called "obsession." He had stopped loving me a long time ago. I was the only fool clinging to the illusion that we could still be happy, still be *a family*.

"I needed this family, Taehyun. I needed you. This life we built together... it was everything to me."

I clenched my fists, my nails digging into my palms.

"And now you're telling me to let it all go? After everything you put me through?"

"Minyoung, stop."

"How can I?" My voice broke. *"I still love you."*

Taehyun shook his head.

"If that's love... I don't want it anymore."

Silence.

A heavy, suffocating silence.

I felt my vision blur. It was over. It was *really* over. The family I fought so hard to keep—gone. My perfect life, my future, slipping through my fingers like sand.

No.

Not like this.

I refused to let it end like this.

I swallowed the lump in my throat and forced a smile.

"Fine." My voice was eerily calm. *"If you want a mutual divorce, I'll give it to you."*

Taehyun blinked, surprised by my sudden compliance.

But even as I spoke those words, one thought burned in the back of my mind.

I'll let you have your divorce.

But I won't let this story end the way you want it to.

Chapter 19: Come Back to Me

I wondered. Maybe if I changed, if I became better, if I did everything right this time—maybe then he'd come back to me.

Yes. It wasn't too late. If I just tried harder, if I became the perfect wife, he would love me again.

So every evening, I prepared a table so full it could barely hold itself up. Every night, I greeted him at the door with a warm smile, pretending like nothing had happened.

"Taehyun, you must be exhausted. I made you a hot meal. Go wash up and eat."

Just like before. Just like the old days, as if nothing had changed.

I watched him as he sat at the table, eating quietly.

Yes, that's it. If I keep doing this every day, he'll realize what he's losing. He'll regret throwing me away.

But that night, he finally spoke.

"Why are you doing this?"

I looked up, still smiling.

"Just giving it my best until the end."

That should make you hesitate. That should make you feel guilty.

You're about to divorce me. You're about to lose me. Shouldn't you feel at least a little regret?

But then, he put his spoon down and looked straight at me.

"Minyoung, find someone who can love you better than I can. You deserve that."

...What?

For a second, my mind went blank.

This wasn't how this was supposed to go.

I thought he'd hesitate. I thought he'd finally say he wasn't sure. I thought he'd tell me he still loved me, that maybe we could work this out.

But instead, he was letting me go. Just like that. As if I was nothing.

I forced a laugh, keeping my voice light.

"Haha... Yeah. You should find someone good too."

But inside, I was seething.

Fine. If I couldn't change his mind directly, I'd go through the people around him.

Who could convince him? Who could remind him that I was good for him, that we belonged together?

Then it hit me. **Dokyung.**

Yes. If anyone could get through to him, it was her.

The next day, I called her.

"Hey, Dokyung. You free? Let's grab a bite. It's been a while."

At the café, she greeted me with a concerned look.

"Minyoung, are you okay?"

"Me? Of course. Why?"

"I don't know... You look exhausted."

Of course, I hadn't been sleeping well. But I brushed it off with a smile, taking a sip of my coffee.

"Dokyung, don't you think Taehyun and I can still work things out?"

She hesitated.

"What do you mean?"

"I mean... If I just try harder, if I prove to him that I've changed, don't you think he'll love me again?"

Dokyung looked at me, her expression unreadable.

"Minyoung... I don't know how to say this, but..."

"What?"

"I think Taehyun... just wants to move on. He's made up his mind."

Move on?

"What do you mean, move on?"

"I mean, he's set on the divorce. He's not changing his mind."

I nodded slowly, keeping my face neutral.

"Ah... I see. Well, that makes sense. For now."

But inside, my stomach churned.

I needed to try harder. I needed more time.

But then, Dokyung sighed.

"Minyoung, I'm not trying to take his side, but... I think you need to find a different way to be happy."

"A different way?"

"Yeah. A fresh start."

A fresh start?

I already knew what would make me happy. **I needed my husband.**

"So... can you just talk to him for me?"

"What?"

"Tell him I've really changed. Tell him to give me another chance."

Dokyung's face hardened.

"Minyoung... I can't do that."

"Why not? We're friends. If you tell him, maybe he'll listen—"

"Minyoung, if I tell him how much you're obsessing over him, I think it'll only push him away more."

The words cut deep.

"Obsessing?"

"I'm sorry, but... this is obsession."

I sat there, gripping my coffee cup.

"I think... it's time to let him go."

I felt a sharp ringing in my ears.

Let him go? End this?

I wasn't done. Not yet.

Chapter 20 : Forever, Just You and Me

If he wouldn't stay with me by choice, then I'd make sure he had no other option.

Love is about staying together, no matter what. Even if one person tries to leave, there should always be a way to make them stay.

I love Taehyun, and he should love me too. That's how it's supposed to be.

So why does he keep trying to run away?

Then, a memory surfaced—an old article I once read online.

Pufferfish poison.

A deadly toxin. But in small amounts, it wouldn't kill—it would just paralyze.

He wouldn't die. He would simply... **lose control.**

Dying wouldn't mean anything to him. But if he came face-to-face with death—if he **felt it creeping up on him**—maybe then, he'd change. Maybe then, he'd realize how much he needed me.

And maybe, just maybe, our relationship could be saved.

I thought about it for a long time.

How much would be enough? Just a little. Just a tiny bit.

That night, I prepared dinner as usual. As I stirred the soup, I carefully extracted **a single drop** of the toxin.

"It's fine. Just a little bit."

I mixed it into a single spoonful of broth. **Just enough.** Not too much. **This wasn't about hurting him—it was about reminding him.**

I set the table, just like always. When Taehyun walked through the door, I greeted him with a smile.

"You're home. You're late today. Hurry up and eat before the soup gets cold."

"You really don't have to do all this."

"I told you, I'll give it my best until the very end. I already made it, so at least eat."

I forced a smile. But inside, my hands were ice-cold.

How would he react? Would he panic? Would he beg me to help him, hold onto me, tell me he'd never leave?

I clenched my sweaty palms as he picked up the spoon.

He took a sip.

And then—

"...This tastes weird."

My heart nearly stopped.

"Huh? What do you mean?"

"I don't know... It's kind of bitter."

I felt the blood drain from my face.

"Oh, I tried a new ingredient. Do you like it?"

"Hmm... I don't know."

He took another sip.

I gripped the edge of the table so tightly my knuckles turned white.

Then, he put his chopsticks down.

"Minyoung."

Something in his voice had changed.

"Did you... do something to this?"

My breath caught in my throat.

"What? What are you talking about?"

"This tastes... really off. And my body feels—"

He stopped mid-sentence. His hand trembled slightly.

At that moment, I knew. **There was no turning back now.**

Chapter 21 : Our True Beginning

Taehyun braced himself against the table, trying to stand. But his knees buckled.

I hid a smile.

That's right. Now, you're finally paying attention to me. Now, you're finally ready to listen.

"Are you okay? Maybe you're just exhausted."

I reached out and gently placed a hand on his shoulder. He tried to shake me off, but his movements were sluggish.

"No... something's wrong. Something's... off."

His eyes widened. Then, he looked at me.

"You... what did you—"

Before he could finish, I shoved him.

Thud!

He collapsed onto the floor, cursing under his breath.

Taehyun tried to push himself up, but his fingers twitched uselessly against the hardwood. His body jerked halfway up before crashing back down.

I slowly knelt beside him. His face was shifting—confusion giving way to fear.

"Taehyun, I told you."

I reached out, stroking his hair.

"We can't just end like this."

"You're insane."

"No."

I smiled.

"For the first time, I think we're finally beginning."

His arm shot out, trying to shove me away, but his strength was failing him.

"Relax, Taehyun. I just want you to stay by my side a little longer."

"What... what did you do?"

"Just a little."

I held up my fingers, barely an inch apart.

"Too much would be dangerous. And I would never let anything happen to you."
He clenched his jaw.
"You're out of your fucking mind."
I softly traced my fingers down his cheek.
"No, Taehyun. I know exactly what I'm doing. You just need to accept it."

Moving him to the bedroom wasn't difficult. The paralysis was spreading, making resistance nearly impossible. He tried to struggle as I pulled him to his feet, but his limbs barely obeyed him.

"Minyoung... don't. Please."

I ignored him.

"You need to rest. That's the only way you'll get better."

I laid him down on the bed and let out a satisfied sigh.

Now, we finally had time. Just the two of us. No distractions. No interruptions.

"You won't get away with this," he rasped.

"Sure. Call the police, then."

I plucked his phone from the nightstand, twirling it in my fingers before casually sliding it into the drawer.

"You can report me when you can actually move."

I walked to the door, locking it from the outside.

Now, no one could take him away from me.

Finally, we could be together.

I leaned against the door and exhaled.

For too long, we'd let outsiders interfere—his family, his friends, his foolish pride.

Not anymore.

"Now, we can finally have a real home."

I whispered the words softly, almost reverently.

"*Now, we can finally be happy.*"

From inside the room, I could hear his ragged breathing, the sound of his body weakly struggling against the inevitable.

"*Just stop fighting, Taehyun.*"

I closed my eyes, resting my forehead against the wood.

"*We're together now. Forever.*"

Chapter 22: Perfect Love

As long as Taehyun behaved, I could be gentle. I brought him food, explained every dose of medicine with a soft voice.

"This will help you feel more comfortable. I don't want you feeling stressed."

"This is just something to help you relax. We wouldn't want you getting too tense, right?"

I cared for him like a devoted nurse. And when he listened, I rewarded him—with a gentle touch on his hair, a spoonful of warm food, a reassuring smile.

"Isn't this nice? Finally, you're really listening to me."

I squeezed his hand.

"No more arguments. No more unnecessary fights. We can live like this, peacefully."

But Taehyun refused to be compliant.

Whenever he was awake, his eyes burned with defiance. He still looked at me like I was his captor, his enemy. I hated that look.

"Why are you looking at me like that?"

Silence.

"I'm doing all of this for us, and you still look at me like that?"

I grabbed his jaw, forcing him to face me.

"Why would you look at someone who loves you this much... like that?"

He clenched his teeth and tried to push me away, but he was too weak. I picked up a glass of water and pressed it against his lips.

"Just relax a little more, okay?"

He tried to resist, spitting the water out, but I gripped his jaw tighter, tilting his head back, forcing him to swallow.

"I told you, don't waste your energy."

Days passed. I took care of him. I spent every moment by his side. And the more time we spent together, the more I felt it—this was what a perfect relationship looked like.

I nurtured him. He stayed by my side.

"This is what marriage should be."

I held his hand, whispering into the quiet room.

"This is what family should feel like."

But then, one day, he spoke even less than usual.

I tilted my head, watching him carefully.

"What's wrong, Taehyun? Why so quiet?"

No response.

I smiled, reaching for his hand.

"You love me, don't you?"

Still, nothing.

I caressed his cheek.

"Taehyun, you love me... don't you?"

Silence.

A slow breath filled my lungs.

"Even after everything I've done for you... you still won't listen?"

I grabbed his jaw, forcing him to meet my gaze.

"Why won't you answer me? After everything I've done for you, you still want to leave?"

His eyes flickered—fear? Guilt? I wasn't sure.

My fingers trembled slightly as I let go.

"We were supposed to be together forever."

I whispered the words like a prayer.

"So why do you keep resisting me?"

Slowly, I rose to my feet, stepping toward the door.

"You just need to relax a little more."

My voice was soft.

"Then you'll finally love me the way I love you."

I turned toward the kitchen. It was time for something stronger.

Chapter 23: Happiness

He no longer resisted—not when I fed him, not when I gave him his medicine.
"You're finally listening to me, Taehyun."
I whispered, stroking his face.
"I knew all we needed was time. Right?"
Taehyun nodded quietly.
A soft, obedient nod.
I smiled, satisfied. He had finally understood—if we were going to stay together, if we were going to protect this marriage, he had to listen.
"Now we're truly one."
I squeezed his hand gently.
"You love me, don't you?"
His lips parted slightly, but no words came out. Instead, he nodded again.
Good.
That was enough.
We could be happy again.

A faint rustling sound woke me from my sleep.
At first, I thought it was part of a dream.
But then, a soft creak. I blinked, slowly sitting up.
The room was dark, but through the gap beneath the door, a faint sliver of light slipped in. And there, silhouetted against it—I saw him.
His hand, gripping the doorknob. Turning it. Quietly.
"...Where are you going?"
My voice was cold. Taehyun's body tensed.
"...Just to the bathroom."
"Don't lie."
I rose from the bed, stepping toward him.

"You were trying to leave."
"No."
"Don't lie to me, Taehyun."
Another step.
"You were trying to run away. You were going to leave me."
He stood frozen, his hand still clutching the knob.
Silence.
Then— In an instant, he yanked the door open. He ran. I lunged, grabbing his arm.
But he was stronger than I expected. He shoved me back, desperate.
"Let go!"
My balance wavered— And then—
THUD. Taehyun stumbled, lost his footing, crashed onto the floor.
His head struck the sharp edge of the bed frame.
For a moment, everything was still. And then—blood.
A slow, dark pool spreading beneath him.
I stared. Frozen. My breath hitched.
"...Taehyun?"
He didn't move. My fingers trembled as I reached out, shaking him.
"Taehyun, are you okay?"
No response.
"Taehyun, stop messing around."
I cradled his face in my hands. But his eyes remained shut.
Panic coiled in my throat. I held my breath, pressing my fingers beneath his nose.
...Breathing. His chest rose and fell, faint but steady.
Alive. Just unconscious. I squeezed my eyes shut.
"It's okay. It's fine."
I whispered, trying to steady my own breathing.
"Taehyun, you just... wanted to rest next to me, right?"
My hands cradled his face, but still—no answer.
What should I do? A hospital?
No.
If I take him there, this will all be over.
If he wakes up and calls the police?

If he leaves me?
If he tells them I'm insane?
No. I can't. I can't. I can't.
I clutched him tighter. My gaze dropped to the floor.
The blood, slowly soaking into the wood beneath him.
His body, limp. His skin, growing colder.
But...
He was still here. With me.
"It's okay. Just sleep a little longer."
I murmured, carefully brushing his hair from his forehead.
He didn't respond.
But that was fine. This time, no one could take him away.
No in-laws, no friends, no stupid pride of his own. No one.
I wrapped my arms around him, pulling him close.
"Now, we finally have time just for us."
My voice was a soft lullaby against his ear.
"Now, we can be together forever."
Tears welled up and spilled down my cheeks.
Not from sadness. No—this was happiness.
Overwhelming, blissful happiness.
"It's okay. It's okay."
I stroked his blood-stained hair, staring into his pale, sleeping face.
"Everything is perfect now."
Just a little longer. Just a little more time.
And he'd finally understand.
That we were perfect just like this.
I smiled.